Contents

A second book of

Aesop's Fables

retold by Marie Stuart

with illustrations by
Robert Ayton

Ladybird Books Ltd Loughborough

The dog and his reflection

One day, a dog took a bone from a shop. He ran off with it before anyone could catch him.

He came to a river and went over the bridge. As he looked down into the water, he saw another dog with a bone!

He did not know that the dog
he saw in the water
was a reflection of himself.

"That dog has a big bone.
It is as big as mine," he said.
"I will jump into the water
and take it from him."

So in he jumped.

When he was in the water,
he could not see the other dog.
And he could not see
the other bone either.

He had lost his own bone, too,
because it fell as he jumped in.

So, because he was greedy,
he got nothing in the end.

Moral :
If you want more because you are greedy, in the end you might find you have less.

The fir tree and the bramble

One day, on a hill top, a fir tree
said to a bramble bush.
"Look at me, I am tall, strong,
graceful and very beautiful.

What good are you?
You are small, ugly and untidy."

This made the bramble bush
very unhappy
because it knew
the fir tree was right.

But next day
some men carrying axes,
came up the hill.

They started to chop down
the fir tree. They wanted to use it
to make a new house.

"Oh dear!" cried the fir tree,
as it started to fall.

"I wish I were a bramble bush,
then the men would not
have cut me down."

Moral:

People who are too proud may be sorry later.

The ant and the dove

One hot day, an ant went
to the river to get a drink of water.
But he fell in and could not get out.

A dove saw that the ant
was in danger.
"I must help him," she said.
"If I pick up this leaf and drop it
in the water, the ant can get on it.
It will be like a little boat."

So the dove
dropped a leaf in the water
and the ant climbed onto it.

"Thank you, Mrs. Dove,"
called the ant.
"I will help you one day."

Soon after, a man came along
with a bow and arrow.
He saw the dove on the tree
and was going to shoot at her.

Just then the ant came along
and bit the man on the leg.

This made the man jump
and his arrow went up into the sky.

The arrow missed the dove,
so she flew away out of danger.

"Thank you little ant,"
cooed the dove.
"You did help me after all."

Moral:
No-one is too little to be helpful.

The boys and the frogs

One day, four boys went out
to play near a pond.

Some frogs lived in the pond.
It was their home.

One bad boy saw the frogs
and said to the other boys,
"Come on! Let's make them jump
out of the water. It will be fun!"

So they all looked for something
to throw at the frogs.

A little frog
saw what they were doing.

He did not like what he saw.

So he hopped onto a floating leaf
in front of the boys.

"STOP!"
shouted the little frog.

"You would not like to have stones
thrown at you if you were frogs.
It may be fun for you,
but it is no fun for us!"

Moral:

*Do not do things to other people
that you would not like done to you.*

The raven and the jug

A big, black raven wanted
a drink.

She saw a big jug with water
at the bottom. She could not
reach the water and wondered
what to do.

"I know" she said.
"I shall put some stones
in the jug. Then the water
will come up to the top."

After the first stone,
the water rose a little.
Then she put in another stone,
and the water rose more.

She put more and more stones in
until the water came up to the top
of the jug.

"Now I can reach the water.
At last I can have a drink,"
said the raven.

So she had a very long drink.

Moral:
*If you try hard enough, you may
find you can do something that at
first seems very difficult.*

The dog in the manger

One day a dog ran into a stable
and jumped into the manger.

The manger had some hay in it.

When the horse and cow
wanted to eat their hay,
the dog would not let them.

"You don't eat hay,
so you don't need it," said the cow.

"We want the hay. It is ours.
It is our dinner," said the horse.

But the dog said,
"If I can't eat it, then I shall not
let you eat it either!"

"Why?" asked the cow.

"Why?" asked the horse.

"Because I don't like to see you eat what I can't eat too," said the dog. "Go away!"

So the horse and the cow had to go away hungry.

Moral:
Do not stop others having what you don't need.

The fox and the grapes

A fox saw some nice grapes.

"They look good," he said.

"I want to eat them,
but they are too high for me.
I must try jumping for them."

He jumped and jumped.

Again and again he jumped
but he could not reach the grapes.

So he said, "I can see now
that they are green.

They are not sweet.

I do not like green grapes.
They are sour. I don't want them."

So he went away without any.

He knew that the grapes
were really very nice.

He just said they were sour
because he could not reach them.

Moral:

It is silly to say that you do not want something just because you cannot have it.

The wolves and the dogs

One day, some wolves said
to some dogs,
"You look like us, why don't you
come and live with us?"

The dogs said,
"We must work for our master
at the farm. He trusts us to help
keep the sheep safe from wolves."

"Why do you work for him?"
said one of the wolves.

"He makes you work hard.
We do not have to work
and we get a lot to eat.
Come away with us,"
said another wolf.

The dogs thought for a long time.
At last they made up their minds.

"Very well," they said.
"We will join you."

So they left the sheep
and went off with the wolves.

When they were far away,
the wolves turned to the dogs
and said,
"Now that we have you here,
we will eat you."

And they did.

Moral:
*Those who cannot be trusted deserve
to be treated badly.*

The fox and the lion

One day a fox saw a lion.

It was the first time he had
ever seen one.

The lion looked so big that the fox
did not know what to do.
He ran away
as fast as he possibly could.

Soon he saw the lion again.

This time the fox said,
"I saw you the other day.
I don't like the look of you. You are
too big. You might want to eat me."

And he ran away again.

As he ran, he said to himself,
"The lion did not eat me last time."

So this time he did not run so fast.

Next day he saw the lion again
and did not run away at all.

"Good morning, Mr. Lion," he said.

"I have seen you before.
You do not look so big today.
I am not afraid of you any more."

So he sat down
to have a long chat with the lion.

Moral:
*Things are not always what they
seem to be at first.*

The bear and the travellers

One day,
two men were on a journey
when they saw a bear.

At first, the bear did not see them.

One man got up into a tree
as fast as he could.

The other man was slow.
"Please help me up," he called.

But the first man went further
up the tree and left him on his own.

"What can I do?"
said the man under the tree.

"If I run away, the bear will see me.
If he sees me, he will eat me."

So he lay on the ground
and did not move.

The bear came up
and walked all round him.

At last it went away.

The man in the tree came down.

He said, "The bear came very close
to you. Did he say anything?"

"Yes," said the other man.
The bear said, "Never go for a walk
with a man who leaves you
when you are in danger."

Moral:
*A real friend will not leave you to
face trouble alone.*

The fox and the stork

One day, a fox said to a stork,
"Would you like to come
to my house for dinner?"

"Yes, please," said the stork.
"That will be very nice."

But when the stork
reached the fox's house, he found
that the fox had put the dinner
on two flat plates.

The stork could not eat anything
because of his long beak.

The fox soon ate his own dinner
and then said to the stork,
"Don't you like your dinner?
If you cannot eat any of it
then I will eat it for you."

So he had his own dinner
and the stork's as well.

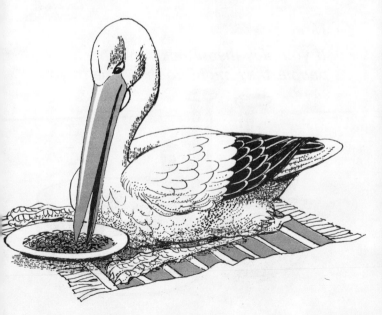

Soon after,
the stork asked the fox to dinner.

The stork put the food in two jugs
which had long necks.

This time it was the fox
who could not reach the food.

He had to watch
while the stork ate both dinners.

Moral:

*If you play mean tricks on other
people, they might do the same to you.*

The man and the partridge

One day, a fat partridge
who was very hungry,
wandered into a bird trap.

She gobbled up the food that was
in the trap and then found
that she could not get out.

The man who had set the trap
arrived soon after.

He was very pleased
to see such a plump bird in his trap.

The partridge was very unhappy
and begged him to let her go.

"Oh please, good sir," she pleaded,
"If you will set me free,
I will lead all my friends
into your trap.
Then you will have
many more birds to eat."

The man took the plump partridge
from his trap and said,
"If you would do that,
then you surely deserve to die.
You are a wicked bird to want
to do such a shameful thing."

Having said this,
he took the partridge home
for his supper.

Moral: *No-one loves a traitor.*

We know very little about Aesop's life in Greece in the 6th Century BC. We believe he was born in Thrace and died about 564 BC. He was probably a slave who was later freed by his master, and was said to be deformed but very clever and witty.

In later years he lived at the court of King Croesus, who sent him on a journey to the Temple of Apollo at Delphi. Here he made the Delphians so angry that they pushed him over a steep cliff to his death.

This carving of Aesop, made in marble, is in the Villa Albani in Rome. It is a copy of a Greek original, probably carved by Lysipus in the 6th Century BC, during Aesop's lifetime.